Walking in Darkness

A vigilante thriller short story
A.K. Hughey

Contents

Chapter One

S helby pulled her beat-up black Civic into a spot at the far end of the gym's parking lot. After turning off the engine, she slid one hand beneath the driver's seat until her fingertips touched the cold steel of a large blade. Her chest relaxed, and her shoulders dropped ever so slightly.

Knowing it was there, just within reach, comforted her. Today was important, and she needed all the reassurance she could get. She inhaled deeply as she opened the car door and stepped out into the cool, wet air. With a twist of the key, Shelby locked her car door before turning and jogging toward the glass doors of the franchise gym.

A blast of hot air greeted her as she entered. She wiped the rain from her eyes and smiled at the young woman standing at the main desk. Flashing her gym card in front of the scanner, she waited for the accepting beep before heading to the locker rooms.

On the way, she hung her car keys at the bottom of the gym's giant, colorful key rack, third hook from the left. After stuffing her hoodie in a locker, Shelby returned to the main room and inserted her earbuds, then shook her hands and rolled her neck. She ignored the nervous tremble in her fingers as she tapped on her workout music playlist. After stepping onto a treadmill, she selected a program for uphill sprints.

She checked her watch again.

7:20 AM.

Only ten more minutes until *he* would arrive. Shelby turned up the speed another two points and tried to burn through her nervous energy.

If her surveillance over the past three weeks had taught her anything about his behavior, he wasn't the type to miss a gym day. He was the type of man who always stuck to a precise schedule. Once he arrived, she'd only have ninety minutes to do what she needed, but she was sure she wouldn't be interrupted.

Shelby alternated between sprinting and jogging on the treadmill, striving to hit new speeds and pushing herself until her calves and thighs burned. Nine minutes in, she changed the program to manual and set the speed to a moderate pace.

Devin walked in through the gym doors at exactly 7:30 a.m.

Right on time. She pretended not to notice, watching him through her peripheral vision.

He hung his keys next to hers, on the second hook from the left, and shoved his stuff in a locker before taking the treadmill next to Shelby's.

She pulled out her earbuds and slowed her speed to a walk.

"There he is, king of the gym," she teased, beaming at him.

"Damn, girl, you worked up a helluva sweat!"

"I'm pushing it. You know I want to own that 10k next month. What are you up to today?"

"A little cardio, then upper body. Are you gonna do pull-ups with me?"

"Not today. I had to come early so I can leave early. I've got a job interview."

"Oh? For what?"

"There's a waitress position open at that little diner on the north side. I need a second job."

"Well, if it doesn't work out, let me know." He locked eyes with her when he spoke, and his words sounded so sincere. She briefly questioned her confidence, barely able to hold her forced smile. "I may have a lead on a great job you'd probably be an excellent fit for."

"Thanks, Devin. I appreciate that." She hit the stop button, then stepped down. "I'll see you tomorrow?"

"You know me. I'll be here."

"I'll take you up on those pull-ups then. Unless they have me start first thing in the morning."

"Well, I hope I'll see you." He beamed at her, and Shelby could feel the charm oozing from his pores. An attractive, blue-eyed man with perfectly messy, medium locks of sandy brown hair. He tried too hard to appear as if he didn't care, but too much product gave away the secret of his vanity. Perfect, straight teeth gleamed from behind lips that many women would kill to kiss.

"You keep on runnin' and hopin'." She winked before turning away and heading for the women's locker room.

Shelby kept her shower short, scrubbing her body and hair as quickly as she could. Anger burned through her as she thought of the wink she'd given him. As much as she hated playing the part, she knew it was a necessary evil. Her doubts faded like smoke in a hurricane as she mentally reviewed the catalyst for her mission.

She had been preparing for this for weeks now, ever since the drunk man, Joe, had shared his glee over the wild weekend he had at Devin's. These weekends didn't involve the usual twenty-year-old male parties. Instead, Devin had procured young women, runaways, and had been holding them captive.

When Joe had turned up with a friend on a Monday night and, over too many shots, spilled the beans about Devin's place, Shelby had made it her mission to track Devin down. She fed Joe too many free shots, flirted with him, and encouraged his loose lips. When Joe's buddy went to the men's room, she encouraged Joe to tell her more about Devin. Believing his tales were exciting her, he didn't hesitate to share how he'd dragged the girls out of their cages, pinning them to the cold floor and forcing himself on them. Biting, scratching, choking. Reveling in their terror-filled eyes and muffled screams.

It had only been a month into her bartending job. Less than two months since her own escape from Phil McNamara's dilapidated farmhouse basement and Lucia's shoot-out with the vile man.

After all she'd been through, she vowed to be braver, to take bolder action sooner. Waiting for someone else to save the other women held in the basement may have gotten them killed. Even if they hadn't yet been murdered, the horrors they would be subjected to daily would rip the hope from their hearts and drain the humanity from their souls. While she had escaped and ran to get help, the girls she'd been held with were moved before the police could save them.

Every day she had to live with the guilt of leaving them, and every night she wrestled with the demons that plagued her, the unwavering regret and the fires of an anger she couldn't quell. Uncovering Devin's secrets and releasing them to the world would be a part of her self-assigned redemption and the focus for all the swells of turmoil within her soul.

Once she had obtained Devin's address and descriptions of what was happening in the basement, she first sent three anonymous tips to the police and waited.

Nothing happened.

When she submitted her final tip and complained, the uninterested operator informed her they couldn't infringe upon his fourth amendment rights without hard evidence.

Shelby could not contain her fury. She railed about the impotence of an anonymous tip system that did not use the tips to save lives. She did her research and found another reason for their inaction could be related to long-term investigations. In such cases, law enforcement would build dossiers full of evidence and trying to get as much information as possible about the key players and chains of command in these criminal organizations before they took action.

While she wanted the cops to get all the monsters involved, Shelby couldn't abide the biggest side effect of long-term case-building: victims held captive were subjected to horrendous sexual abuse and torture until they were rescued.

What good was a solid case if a kid was put in the "damage group" and died after being sold forty or fifty times a day? What good was a solid case when the laws and sentencing against traffickers were so lenient? What good was the legal system when the pimps got out on good behavior? Even after they had raped and tortured their victims and threatened to kill their families if the victims dared try to escape?

Shelby didn't see why people who had no souls should be allowed to live, especially freely. She didn't know if she was ready to pull the trigger herself, but this wasn't the mission where she would find out. Too much could go wrong in the quiet, suburban neighborhood. For the time being, she would do what she could to help speed along saving the women being held in Devin's basement. She couldn't live with herself if she left it to the cops, making them live in a daily hell for months or years while the cops built a case.

No. She was committed.

If the cops wouldn't do anything, she would.

And after Shelby handled Devin and his basement, she would have something special in store for Joe, too.

Chapter Two

She dressed quickly after her shower and examined herself in the full-length mirror. Black, form-fitting slacks and a cream-colored satin blouse were perfect attire for a job interview.

So plain, so ordinary. So inconspicuous, yet distracting to those who would find her form attractive. She never thought of herself as pretty. There was too much damage burning in the eyes that stared back at her from the mirror. She didn't know if she would ever look into them and smile again.

But Shelby knew what other people liked to see in a woman. They liked a small waist, a round butt, and a lifted bust. She pulled her dark, straightened hair back into a low ponytail and tucked the loose front locks behind her ears.

If she conformed to expectations, it was a hell of a lot easier to gain trust and go unnoticed. It was also much easier to fulfill her newfound purpose in life. The ability to quickly build rapport and go unnoticed when needed were skills crucial to her success—and survival.

Shelby exited the women's locker room, gym bag slung over her left shoulder. Her stomach flipped when she spotted Devin. He was still on the treadmill. Another ten minutes of cardio, then he'd spend forty-five minutes lifting and another five minutes chatting with his buddies before heading home. When she retrieved her keys from the board, she deftly swiped his keys as well.

She couldn't stop herself from glancing back at Devin. He focused on his run, sprinting and pushing for that next level as he always did. The man was a beast in the gym, rippling with muscles and towering over her at an intimidating 6'1".

She could only imagine what kind of hell she would be in for if he knew what she was up to.

Shelby waved with her free hand to the attendant half asleep at the front desk as she walked out of the gym. The cold, humid air hit her warm cheeks like a slap. Each drop of cold rain from the fat, dark-gray clouds snapped against her skin. She worried as she hurried across the parking lot and prayed there wouldn't be snow within the hour.

If she had the luxury of more time, she might have checked her weather app again to see if the forecast had changed, but she needed to stay on task. It was all she could do to keep herself from sprinting to her car.

The drive was short, but Shelby spent all ten minutes reviewing her plan to break into Devin's house. Although she had never been to his house before, she had made it a point to talk with him about home renovation. She started the line of conversation by discussing her own DIY improvements of her old Victorian on Main Street. Being a bit of a narcissist, he couldn't resist the opportunity to talk about his own place and stake a position of authority on the matter, over-explaining the simplest of jobs. Shelby didn't own an old Victorian, but the one she had mentioned was a favorite of hers, and she had no intention of telling him where she actually lived.

Bit by bit, she had gotten him to talk about every inch of his home. He had described every single room in excessive detail. Every room, that is, except the basement.

"It's unfinished," he would say, his suddenly sullen expression telling her the space was in a state contrary to his standards, despite his pride. His wealth was more than sufficient to finish it as he was a young, single, highly experienced freelance application programmer.

According to his fellow dirtbags, the basement, her target today, was where he kept his secrets.

Shelby pulled her car into the parking lot of an abandoned auto shop. It was one of the few places she could find within walking distance of Devin's house that wasn't covered by security cameras. It also provided almost direct access to Devin's backyard.

After setting the parking brake and killing the engine, she pulled her blouse over her head and quickly changed out of her interview clothes. In their place, she slipped into dark blue skinny jeans, warm socks, winter boots, and a black turtleneck sweater.

Cars sped past on the road next to the shop. She released her thick black hair and smoothed it into a low bun before removing a blonde wig from beneath the passenger seat. Carefully, she pinned it in place. The wavy locks almost appeared natural and completely covered her real hair. She improved the look by covering her exposed skin with a light-toned liquid foundation, then added a layer of dark pink lipstick to her mouth. A pair of oversized sunglasses finished her look.

Her mixed ethnicity allowed her to alter her appearance and conceal her true identity easily. Today, she would be a slim Caucasian girl in case a neighbor witnessed her walking into Devin's place.

Shelby tugged on black suede winter driving gloves before pulling one of a dozen burner phones out of the glove compartment. Next, she grabbed a black plastic garbage bag from the passenger side floorboard and opened it fully before leaving it under the brake pedal.

Taking a deep breath to fill her diaphragm, she held it for five seconds before slowly exhaling. She'd learned the de-stressing exercise from an article by a former Navy SEAL and had ingrained it into her daily practices. Shelby continued her controlled, deep breathing to still her nerves as she climbed out of the car.

Holding Devin's keys in one hand, she slid her phone into a back pocket of her jeans and glanced at her watch.

Fifty minutes remained.

After rounding the abandoned building, Shelby made her way through the prickly, dead, overgrown grass toward a tall wooden fence. In the summer, the vegetation would have whispered at her passing. But now, on the cusp of winter, the stalks of tall grass and weeds cracked with her every step despite the near-constant rain that should have softened them. In that moment, she no longer regretted her decision to pony up the extra dollars for water-proof makeup.

She approached the rotted section of the planks she had found and kicked out last week. Careful to keep her clothes clean and wig in place, she ducked low and slid through the tiny opening. Her jeans quickly became soaked by the tall, wet grass. Yet she was grateful for the overgrowth. The dead vegetation was thick enough to keep her from splashing mud and carrying it with her. She didn't want to help any potential investigators more easily track her path of ingress and egress.

A narrow, grassy pathway led between the fenced backyards of quiet family homes that stretched out before her. The houses were built close together, and Shelby knew anyone could be watching her. Still, her current approach would be less conspicuous than walking up to the front door, and she also wouldn't be recorded on anyone's doorbell camera.

Shelby walked comfortably, not too fast and not too slow. She was betting on someone seeing her, and she wanted to appear as if she belonged here. She hadn't ever truly felt like she belonged anywhere, but that was a dark train of thoughts for another time. It would be a night spent alone in her apartment, with only a tall bottle of bourbon for company.

Her skin tingled and her muscles ached with tension, mind racing through what she would do if someone called out to her or approached.

Finally, she reached Devin's gated backyard. A six-foot-tall fence surrounded it, blocking much of the view from the ground. Once she was out of the narrow pathway, the fencing would conceal her presence. Slipping her hand in her pocket, she wrapped her fingers around his keys and pulled them out.

A loud metal crash stopped Shelby, and she nearly dropped the keys as she yanked her hand free of her pocket to defend herself.

Chapter Three

S he wheeled around, hands up and ready to fight. Searching for
the source of the noise, she found a small, black and white cat
leaping away from a pile of metal debris behind a nearby house. The
cat had jumped on a rusted trash can, causing the metal lid to slip off
before hitting the pavement and crashing against the can.

She cursed under her breath and spun the keys in her fingers. Others
may have heard the sound, but she didn't dare look around to see.
It would instantly mark her as out of place. Instead, she quickly and
carefully selected the key she hoped was right before slipping it into
the lock.

Turning it in the heavy padlock, she silently thanked the heavens
when it popped open. Her heart thudded in her chest as she stepped
through the gate and latched it behind her. Knowing Devin kept
cameras on his entrances and in his house, she kept her head down
and let the bangs of her wig fall over her eyes and face, the long, wavy
strands clinging to her cold cheeks.

Without the right hair color or a clear shot of the shape of her face
and eyebrows, it would be difficult for anyone to identify her without
additional corroborating pieces of evidence—especially in such a small
town. The suede gloves covering her hands ensured she would not
leave fingerprints. She was careful to make sure her clothes were metic-
ulously clean and free of loose strands of her real hair, but there was
always the chance she would leave some evidence that forensic techs

could find. After doing as much as possible to prevent that, she could only hope and pray that crucial evidence of her activities wouldn't be left behind.

She unlocked the backdoor and quietly slipped inside. She stopped to steady herself and took several deep, calming breaths to slow her racing heart. Adrenaline pumped through her veins, her senses sharpening and her hands trembling as she surveyed her surroundings.

An open kitchen greeted her, and it was just as he described: cherrywood cabinets, gleaming granite countertops, and spotless black appliances. A pendant light hung over a small island where all the ingredients for his morning protein shake waited for him.

Quietly, out of habit rather than necessity now that she was inside, Shelby pulled the burner phone from her back pocket and turned it on. Once it was fully functioning, she turned on the GPS and location functions and took pictures around the house. She switched to video recording, beginning with the front door and moving toward the back door through the living room and dining room. She stopped the recording and started again from the kitchen, making her way to the basement door. Her slender fingers unlocked the door and opened it wide with one hand while she continued recording.

She turned on the light switch at the top of the stairs and hesitated only briefly. If what Joe had described was real, what she found in the basement might look too much like her own trauma. Would she freeze? Would PTSD stop her from completing her mission as intended? Or could she push through and overcome her trauma to save others?

Worse: What if she was wrong and found nothing?

Shelby shook her head.

No. She was confident in her instincts, her intuition, and the veracity of Joe's claims.

Her right foot hovered over the first step, then slowly lowered. She grabbed the stair railing with her free hand and kept the camera steady as she descended. Despite her careful, slow steps, her boots still thunked on the unfinished wood as she descended. Another light switch awaited her at the bottom of the stairs.

He starves them, she remembered hearing Joe tell his friends. So, when we're ready, they do whatever we want.

Shelby swallowed her fear and flipped the switch.

Chapter Four

S helby's breath caught in her chest when the flickering fluorescent lights came to life and illuminated Devin's secrets.

There were four large dog crates, the wire kind meant to keep big dogs from destroying the house out of loneliness. Instead of dogs, each of the crates held a young woman. They were all barely covered by dirty, small blankets. There wasn't enough room to fully stand or stretch out. One of them whimpered and lifted her head, the light waking her.

Shelby's chest tightened as she held up the phone and panned the camera around the dingy, unfinished basement. She fought to keep her hand steady and her voice silent.

She glanced at her watch.

Twenty-five minutes left.

She needed to get out of here soon to change her clothes, wipe away all the foundation and lipstick, and return Devin's keys to the board in the gym before he was ready to leave.

"Help," the starved woman croaked, her voice scratchy and dry. "Please help us."

Her skin was dirty and bruised, hair matted and greasy. Patches were missing. Shelby's stomach rolled as she imagined how she likely lost those patches of hair. A swollen bottom lip sporting dried blood quivered as she waited for Shelby to say something.

Shelby brought a gloved finger to her mouth to indicate silence.

The woman didn't seem to understand. Instead of seeing hope come alive in her eyes, Shelby watched it flicker and die.

The woman, her arms quaking with the effort of pushing herself up to lock eyes with Shelby, simply collapsed. The dirty blanket muffled her quiet sobs.

Shelby ended the recording and returned to the home screen. She had almost full signal, which she hadn't expected in the basement, considering all the security measures Devin had bragged about. A cell phone signal jammer wasn't on his equipment list, and he had exaggerated his implements. There wasn't even a security system to deal with.

Since the GPS signal indicator on the phone was active, Shelby texted the videos to the officers whose phone numbers she had collected through less than honest methods. Then she crouched down close to the girl who had tried to talk to her.

"Take this," she whispered, pushing the cell phone through the wire. "He won't be back for at least twenty-five minutes. Wait five minutes, then call 9-1-1. Can you do that?"

"Let me out," the girl pleaded as tears poured down her cheeks.

Shelby closed her eyes and shook her head. "If you want him nailed to the wall, you need to get the cops here. They need to see all of this. That's the only way..." Her words trailed off as she remembered what Joe had described doing to these girls. "Don't leave them behind." Shelby gestured to the others.

"Never," the girl whispered in horror as she wiped away the tears with the back of her hand. She opened the home screen and stared in disbelief. "It works!"

"I came to help, but I need to leave now. Can you do this?"

The girl hesitated for a moment, eyeing her suspiciously. Shelby stared deep into the other woman's eyes. Aside from suspicion, there was also a glimmer of hope.

Shelby checked her watch again, anxious to be on her way. She knew there were families out there who thought these girls had run away or been killed. Families that still hoped and prayed for a safe return, fighting sleep for the nightmares that would haunt them as they imagined what their children might be enduring out in the big, dark world.

"Please stay until the cops come," the young woman begged.

"I can't. I'm not supposed to be here. Can you do it?" Shelby hissed. She kept her words gentle and low, careful to conceal her true voice.

The girl's trembling lips parted, but she didn't speak. "What's your name?" Shelby whispered.

"Daria," the girl said, choking back a sob.

Shelby glanced at her watch again, too nervous to read the time. "Daria, I came here to help, but I can't be seen here. I need time to get out."

"B-but what if he comes back first?" Her terror-filled eyes could only hint at the hell she'd been through.

Shelby hadn't been held captive as long as this girl likely had, but she'd still been raped, beaten, and had the hope ripped out of her soul.

The other girls stirred. Shelby knew Daria was terrified that something might go wrong before the cops could come, and she couldn't blame her.

"Fine, just dial now," Shelby conceded.

Although she had planned to have a few minutes to be sure she was well away before the cops came, she couldn't bear the thought of something going wrong and leaving these women to more torture and abuse. Being caught with a phone might mean dismemberment and death for them.

The woman opened the screen, the glint of hope in her eyes turning to fire as she double-checked the signal.

"What if it doesn't work?" Fresh tears filled her eyes as she breathed the words. She tapped the numbers 9-1-1 then touched the phone icon before bringing it to her ear.

"It will work," Shelby whispered before turning and heading for the stairs. "I need to go."

She was about to turn the light off, but her hand hovered over the switch.

One way or another, this was all coming to a head. Soon, the police would know the young women were here, so it didn't matter if Shelby returned everything to the state in which it was found. At least not this time.

No. She wouldn't leave them trapped in darkness any longer.

As Shelby neared the top of the stairs, she heard the young woman whispering, likely talking to an operator.

Another noise made her freeze in place, chilling her blood. A door closed on the main floor, and footsteps thudded slowly over the hardwood floors.

Chapter Five

I t took every ounce of Shelby's discipline not to run down the stairs.

Without taking her eyes from the stairwell, she carefully retraced her steps, backing soundlessly down the stairs.

"Devin," a man called out. "You home?"

Shelby instantly recognized Joe's voice. She ground her teeth as she reached the basement floor and hid behind the walled stairwell.

His steps sounded on the stairs as she waited in the cold shadows, mentally flipping through the backup plans she had devised. She hadn't wanted to admit it, but she had counted on this first mission going smoothly without encountering any other people aside from the victims.

"Are you feeding your pets?" Joe asked as he neared the bottom. "Or playing?"

Shelby's muscles quivered, and the bile rose in her throat. She was disgusted and reminded of her own ordeal only a couple of months earlier.

How can such monsters live with themselves? She wished evil men like him could be more easily identified and sent straight to hell.

She listened as he paused at the bottom of the stairs.

"Devin?" he called again, more weakly this time. He muttered something else to himself that she couldn't hear.

By Shelby's estimate, Joe would soon get suspicious and call Devin if he didn't see his friend.

Five, four, three, she counted silently.

"Where in the hell did you get that?" Joe shrieked. Keys jangled, and his boots slapped against the pavement as he rushed toward the cages.

Two, one... go!

Shelby exhaled a breath, then stepped out silently from her hiding place behind the stairwell. Joe crouched in front of the cage, unlocking the padlock before swinging the door open and leaning in. He reached forward and tried to wrench the phone from Daria's hands, but her bony fingers desperately gripped it.

Daria looked behind Joe as Shelby hovered behind him. She wasn't foolish enough to get in the cage with him, even if there had been enough room, but Daria's distracted gaze was enough to get his attention. He glanced over his shoulder at Shelby and did a double-take.

"What the he–" He tried to stand, apparently forgetting he was in a dog crate, and smashed his neck against the opening. The hit to his neck sent him to his hands and knees.

Shelby reached in and dragged him out by his coat. A sharp piece of wire scratched his face as she flung him backward, strong from months of hatred-fueled training. She kicked him viciously in the face.

Joe's head snapped back, and he slumped only briefly before an adrenaline-fueled scramble against a support post. Blood dripped from his mouth as he stood, squaring off with her, his eyes filled with fury.

This was not the happy, carefree drunk she'd seen at the bar. The monster was now revealed in the empty, cold depths of his green eyes.

"You're dead, bitch," he growled before bending at the hips and rushing her like a defensive lineman.

She wasn't fast enough to feint, taking the hit instead and digging her nails into his neck as they went down. Shelby sputtered, her wig flying from her head as her back hit the cement floor, Joe landing between her legs. He reached forward across her chest, pulling back and putting his neck out of her reach, then wrapping his strong fingers around her throat.

Instinct told her to fight and get his hands off her neck, so her nails clawed at the sleeves of his coat as she tried to push his arms away.

Shelby's vision was fading fast when she stilled her mind for a fraction of a second, closing her eyes and remembering what she'd trained for.

In a split second, she pushed against Joe's sternum with her hands, simultaneously pulling her legs to her chest. She created a little more space between them before kicking forward with everything she had.

Her dominant right leg hit first, impacting his trachea. He sputtered, his eyes going wide as her left foot pounded his chest and flung him backward. Gasping for breath, Joe fell back onto the cement, massaging his throat with his fingers, eyes wide with panic.

As the oxygen returned to her head, Shelby heard the terrified cries of the young women in the cages. She looked up, her vision clearing, and studied their tear-streaked faces. Fists pounded against the walls of the crates, and Daria called to her.

It took Shelby several moments to understand what Daria was repeating.

"Finish him," Daria insisted, her tone cold and deadly, despite its nervous tremble.

Shelby turned her gaze back on Joe. He was sucking in deeper breaths now, recovering from the blow to his throat. If she'd had a little more space before kicking him, she might have finished him then. As it stood now, he might recover from his injuries.

As he crawled to his hands and knees, Shelby hauled her leg back and kicked his head as hard as she could.

He went sprawling onto his back, moaning unintelligibly while gripping his head with both hands.

If he recovered, he could do more than just come after her. He could identify her by name to the police when they showed up.

The cops!

Her quaking stopped as the realization hit her.

How much time had passed since Daria had started her conversation with the operator?

She whipped her head around to lock eyes with Daria, who was still. Tears streamed down her cheeks, and darkness filled her eyes.

Shelby watched as Daria tapped the red button, ending the 9-1-1 call. She crawled out of the cage and grimaced as she stood and stretched.

"Finish him," she repeated, the phone hanging in her hands. "Or I will."

Breaking eye contact, Shelby grabbed the keys Joe had left in the padlock on the crate that had held Daria. She then unlocked the other cages.

"Do you know what he's done to us?" Daria sobbed, pointing to a bald patch on her head and baring her teeth. Several were broken or missing.

Shelby swallowed hard and carefully took the phone from Daria's hand. She unlocked the screen, tapped 9-1-1 in the Recents menu to re-initiate the call, and hit the speaker button.

"You'll sleep better if you do it yourself," Shelby whispered as the call connected, knowing from her own experience. She could only dream now of extracting justice from her captors and rapists. "He's all yours." Shelby pointed to Joe with her free hand. "You might have a couple of minutes to make sure he can never do this to anyone else ever again."

A ring sounded over the phone hanging from her hands. She bent down and placed it on the cement. It rang one more time before someone answered. "9-1-1, what is your emergency?"

Shelby picked up her wig from the floor and headed for the stairs. Glancing back as she took the first step, she witnessed Daria strike first, viciously kicking Joe in the head before the other girls joined in.

Chapter Six

B y the time Shelby reached the top of the stairs, she could hear the girl talking to an operator. She pulled the keys from the basement door and left it wide open, the echoes of the women in the basement growing softer as Shelby walked away.

She passed through the backdoor and closed it behind her, careful to appear calm to any neighbors who might be watching. The soft hairs of the blonde wig tickled her cheeks, but she didn't brush them away; the stray locks would help conceal her face.

It was all she could do to keep herself from running as she locked the gate to the backyard and turned down the narrow path between the fences. Her skin crawled and prickled. Someone was watching her. She could feel it, but she didn't dare turn her head.

Holding her wig in place with one hand, she ducked through the hole in the fence near the abandoned auto shop and slid through. Her muscles flexed and tensed as she walked to her car. She took off her boots before climbing in, satisfied that the angle of the building and unusual height of the fence had covered her exit.

Shelby shoved the boots into a black garbage bag along with the wig, winter socks, and her clothes before putting on her interview outfit again. She pulled the elastic tie from her hair and let it loose. Makeup removing wipes cleared away the foundation, and she wiped off the red lipstick, replacing it with coconut lip balm.

Once her appearance mostly matched her pre-breaking-and-entering look, she shifted the Civic into first. She waited at the edge of the drive until a group of vehicles came along the roadway.

She turned right onto the road after them and caught up quickly, then zipped between the cars and trucks until she was in the middle of the gaggle on the four-lane boulevard. She wasn't returning to the gym the same way she had come, and she needed her car to blend into traffic as much as possible in case the police examined the security footage from local businesses for suspects.

Certainly, the girl would probably mention Shelby, and the police might seek this mystery person. Shelby didn't want to be found, and she couldn't live her purpose if she was discovered. She'd already told the cops what she had heard, and they had done nothing about it.

While they had done nothing, Shelby had claimed her first victory

Shelby focused on calming herself as she pulled back into the gym parking lot. She couldn't unsee the teen girls in the cages, their bruised faces and sunken cheeks. The living horror in the girls' eyes burned bright in Shelby's mind as she walked back into the gym and scanned her card at the desk.

As smoothly as possible, she hung her keys and Devin's keys next to each other on the board, just where they had been before she had swiped both sets. She didn't bother searching the gym for him. Instead, she headed to the bathroom to touch up her appearance. In whispers, she stared into the mirror and practiced what she would say to him, closely studying her eye movements and the way her cheeks twitched when she lied.

After a few minutes of practice, Shelby was satisfied with her fake smile and believed she had tamed her eyes and her face so they wouldn't tell on her.

When she exited the bathroom, she found Devin doing bench presses in the strength section. He was doing reps with two 45s and a 10 on each side. The man spotting him rippled with muscle, a stereotypical jock. His sharp-angled jaw and stony eyes warned her against intruding.

She stood nearby and waited until Devin finished his set. After sitting up and taking a few ragged breaths, he spotted her. She waved and walked closer.

"Hey," he said with a grin. "You're back?"

"I got the job!" The relaxed, cheerful smile she had practiced came more easily this time. What she had seen in the basement had steeled her against Devin and his deceptive public persona.

"Congrats! I guess this means I won't get to see you tomorrow?"

"Well, that's the best part. I don't start until next Monday. Then I'll work mornings. But at least we'll have the rest of the week together." She brushed a lock of hair behind her ear and intentionally softened her expression.

Demure, she reminded herself.

"I guess once you start next week, we'll have to find another time to hang out. Would that be all right?" He wore that signature grin, the one that probably made most women's knees turn to jelly. She forced her smile wider and played along as if he had that effect on her now.

"I'd like that." She pulled a slip of paper from her pocket and handed it to him. "I'm going to plan something this weekend to celebrate the new job. Let me know if you're up for a night out."

"I think I can clear my calendar to help you celebrate." He gave her a wink before opening the paper and glancing at her name and number.

"Well, I better get out of this." She gestured to her slacks and blouse. "I'll see you tomorrow morning. Usual time?"

"As usual," he agreed. "I can't wait."

"Me too." She winked before turning on her heel and walking out. Taking advantage of the kitten platform pumps, she swayed her hips in the way she knew a man like him would enjoy. If she played it right, his thoughts of her would distract as he made his way home. If the cops weren't already there, they would be shortly.

Shelby grabbed her keys and left the gym, waving to the woman reading a magazine behind the desk as she pushed through the doors and walked out into the rain once more. She didn't even mind the bitter drops nipping at her exposed skin anymore.

Back in the driver's seat of her car, she turned on a playlist of her favorite Rihanna songs and sang along at the top of her lungs as she drove back to her apartment.

That night, as she tended bar at Ginger's, Shelby tried not to smile when the evening news announced the recovery of four missing teenage girls. The reporters shared that two of the missing girls were from Detroit, one from Chicago, and the fourth was from Indianapolis. Devin's mugshot was front and center as they described a seemingly normal young man with a "den of dark secrets."

"I don't think anyone saw this coming," the male anchor stated to his female counterpart.

"It's just scary," the woman replied simply, shaking her head in disbelief.

A tension that Shelby hadn't realized she was carrying slowly released from her chest, and she could finally breathe again. The thought of Devin surrounded by far scarier men almost made her chuckle. At least until another picture flashed on the screen.

"Police have also released this sketch of a person of interest." A sketch of a blonde woman with a square face and big sunglasses filled the TV. "If you have any information, please call the number at the bottom of your screen."

Shelby's tension melted away as she realized the costume had done its job. Without makeup, her skin was too dark to match the description, and the expensive, natural-looking wig had successfully concealed the angles of her face.

After she'd served all three of her regulars, Shelby asked the barback to take over while she stepped outside. In front of the little dive bar, she smoked a cigarette while watching giant, chunky snowflakes float down from the darkened heavens. Although the town was small, there was enough light to cast an orange glow on the underbelly of the thick snow clouds lingering above.

Thinking of Mel and the other girls she'd been held with, the ones she hadn't been able to save, she vowed again—just as she had vowed every night since she left them—that she would make up for her mistakes. She would help others until she could find them.

Although this was the first time she'd taken direct action to free others, Shelby basked in the satisfaction of a successful mission. She rolled the ember from her cigarette and dropped it onto the cold pavement. Pressing the toe of her boot into it, she crushed the burning tobacco beneath her foot, the same foot she'd kicked Joe's head with. The gritty crunch vibrated through her leg as she thought of the girls. Their terror, she prayed, would now be over, and they could begin to heal. For Shelby, this was only the beginning of her journey. She had her purpose now, and she would fulfill it until she drew her final breath.

Read More

In chronological order:

- Desecrate the Darkness - Book 1

- Walking in Darkness - Standalone short story available on Amazon.

- Stand Against Darkness - Standalone short story.

    - Would you like to read it for FREE? Head to www.akh ughey.com/freestand

- Hunting Darkness - Short story originally featured in the Make Them Pay thriller anthology.

    - Would you like to read it for FREE? Head to www.akh ughey.com/freehunt

- Together Against Darkness - Short story featured in the March For Justice anthology.

- Falling Into Darkness - Book 2

- Rising From Darkness - Book 3

Would you like updates about upcoming releases, live events, giveaways, and reader parties?

- Join my Dark Angels Reader Bulletin at akhughey.com.

- Get access to Bonus Content like flash fiction, more short stories, books, audio, and more when you join me on Ream: https://reamstories.com/shadowsandscreams

About the Author

Writing became A.K.'s passion from a young age, her notebooks quickly filling with high fantasy and science fiction short stories. What began as fiction writing evolved to consist mostly of report writing and formal business communication during her fourteen years of active and reserve duty in the United States Army. While pursuing her Bachelor of Arts in English with a concentration in Writing, she began contributing regularly to non-fiction magazines and first saw her byline in print in July of 2015.

After attaining her B.A. in English (Writing) and completing her M.A. in Ancient and Classical History, she has returned her focus to completing her many writing projects.

Connect with A.K. Hughey

Website: www.akhughey.com
Ream: https://reamstories.com/shadowsandscreams
Facebook: www.facebook.com/audreyiswriting
Instagram: www.instagram.com/audreyiswriting
Twitter: www.twitter.com/audreyiswriting
TikTok: www.tiktok.com/@audreyiswriting

www.ingramcontent.com/pod-product-compliance
Lightning Source LLC
Chambersburg PA
CBHW020611130626
46552CB00007B/3145